Trailblazers

FOOTBALL★ FACTOR

GOAL MACHINE

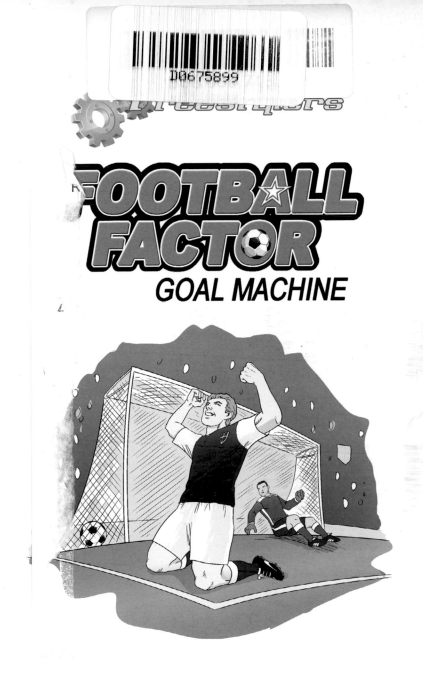

First published in 2013 by Wayland

Text copyright © Alan Durant 2013
Illustrations © Wayland 2013

Wayland
338 Euston Road
London NW1 3BH

Wayland Australia
Level 17/207 Kent Street
Sydney, NSW 2000

Series Editor: Victoria Brooker
Series design: Robert Walster and Basement68
Cover design: Lisa Peacock
Consultant: Dee Reid

A CIP catalogue record for this book is available
from the British Library.
Dewey number: 823.9'2-dc23

ISBN 978 0 7502 7982 6

2 4 6 8 10 9 7 5 3 1

Printed in China

Wayland is a division of Hachette Children's Books,
an Hachette UK Company
www.hachette.co.uk

FOOTBALL FACTOR

GOAL MACHINE

Alan Durant and Andrew Chiu

WAYLAND

www.waylandbooks.co.uk

"Goal!"

Naz scored again for Sheldon Rovers.

He was on top form.

It was his sixteenth goal of the season.

Dave Brown, Sheldon's manager,
called Naz 'The Goal Machine'.

"You'll play for England one day,"
he said. Naz grinned.

"Thanks, boss," he said.

The next game Naz didn't score.
Twice the goalie made great saves.

Then Naz hit the post … and the bar.

"Bad luck, Naz," said Kyle, who was
Sheldon Rover's captain.

Naz had bad luck in the next match too.
He scored, but it was offside.

In the last minute Naz missed
an easy goal. Sheldon Rovers
lost 1- 0. Naz lost confidence.
It was all going wrong.

"You're trying too hard," said Dave Brown.
"So I'm giving you a rest."

Naz was a sub for the next match.

It was the third round of the Cup.

Naz was gutted.

On match day Naz sat on the bench.

He looked into the crowd.

He couldn't believe it!

The England manager was in the crowd! And Naz wasn't playing! Now he was really gutted.

Sheldon's right winger, Danny, scored. But the other team scored too. At half-time it was 1-1.

Sheldon missed some good chances.

Robby took a heavy tackle.

He had to come off.

"You're on, Naz," said the manager.
Naz was very nervous. He wanted to play
well in front of the England manager.

Sheldon had a corner. Danny kicked
a high ball across to Naz. Naz leapt.
He was right in front of the goal.
He couldn't miss.

But he did!

He headed the ball over the bar.

The crowd groaned.

Naz put his head in his hands.

"Head up, Naz!" called Kyle.

Naz had another chance of a goal.
He hit his shot early.
Somehow the keeper saved it!
The crowd groaned again.

There were two minutes left.

Sheldon had another corner.

Naz swung his boot at the ball.

He missed it completely and fell over.

The ball went across the goal.

Kyle kicked it back. Thump!

"Agh!" Naz cried out.

"Goal!" shouted the crowd.

The Sheldon players jumped on Naz.

"What's going on?" he said.

"The ball hit your bum and went in," laughed Kyle.

Soon after the restart Kyle won the
ball. He slid a pass to Naz.

Naz took the ball in his stride.
Bang! He thumped it into the net.

Sheldon Rovers had won 3–1.
They were in the quarter finals.

Kyle gave Naz a high five.

"Well done, Naz," he said.

Joe Ford, the Sheldon coach, slapped Naz on the back.

"You were due some luck, Goal Machine," he said.

"Luck?" said Naz. He wagged his backside. "That was pure skill!" He grinned. "I hope the England manager was watching…"

Read more stories about Sheldon Rovers.

Sheldon Rovers have made it to the Cup final. It is their manager Dave Brown's last match. Will Danny, Robby, Naz, Ledley and Tom play their best? Can they make Dave's day and win the Cup?

Danny is playing his first match for Sheldon Rovers. It is the first round of the Cup. He needs to play well to keep his place. But will nerves get the better of him?

Naz is Sheldon Rover's top scorer. He is a goal machine. But suddenly things start to go wrong. He can't score at all. He loses his place in the team. Will he ever get his goal touch back?

Tom plays in goal for Sheldon Rovers. He has a lucky horseshoe that he takes to every match. But on Cup semi-final day it goes missing. Things start to go wrong. Has Tom's luck run out?

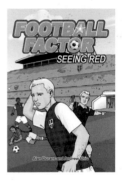

Robby keeps getting sent off. Now he has got a three-match ban and he feels down. Can he learn to control his temper? Will he ever get back in the team?

Ledley is a defender for Sheldon Rovers. He has been out injured for months. His first game is the Cup quarter final. Will he last the game? Will his tackling be strong enough?

FOR TEACHERS

About Freestylers

Freestylers is a series of carefully levelled stories, especially geared for struggling readers of both sexes. With very low reading age and high interest age, these books are humorous, fun, up-to-the-minute and edgy. Core characters provide familiarity in all of the stories, build confidence and ease pupils from one story through to the next, accelerating reading progress.

Freestylers can be used for both guided and independent reading. To make the most of the books you can:

- Focus on making each reading session successful. Talk about the text before the pupil starts reading. Introduce the characters, the storyline and any unfamiliar vocabulary.

- Encourage the pupil to talk about the book during reading and after reading. How would they have felt if they were one of the characters playing for Sheldon Rovers? How would they have dealt with the situations that the players found themselves in?

- Talk about which parts of the story they like best and why.

For guidance, this story has been approximately measured to:

National Curriculum Level: 1B   ATOS: 1.5
Reading Age: 6   Lexile ® Measure [confirmed]: 280L
Book Band: Orange